Choosing a Career in Aircraft Maintenance

Although much of the glory in the airline industry goes to the pilots, it is the work of the aircraft mechanics that makes planes fly safely.

Choosing a
Career in
Aircraft
Maintenance

Amy Sterling Casil

INSTRUCTIONAL MEDIA CENTER
GRISSOM MIDDLE SCHOOL
MISHAWAKA, INDIANA

The Rosen Publishing Group, Inc.
New York

To the students and teachers at the aircraft maintenance program at San Bernardino Valley College and all AMTs and mechanics everywhere

Published in 2002 by The Rosen Publishing Group, Inc.
29 East 21st Street, New York, NY 10010

Copyright © 2002 by The Rosen Publishing Group, Inc.

First Edition

Library of Congress Cataloging-in-Publication Data

Casil, Amy Sterling.
Choosing a career in aircraft maintenance / by Amy Sterling Casil.—
1st ed.
p. cm.—(World of work)
Includes bibliographical references and index.
ISBN 0-8239-3567-1 (library binding)
1. Airplanes—Maintenance and repair—Vocational guidance—Juvenile
literature. [1. Airplanes—Maintenance and repair—Vocational
guidance. 2. Vocational guidance.] I. Title. II. World of work (New
York, N.Y.)
TL671.9 .C35 2001

2001002359

Manufactured in the United States of America

Contents

Introduction

Who hasn't watched a jet fly overhead and felt the wonder and beauty of flight? Flying has captured the imagination of millions ever since the Wright brothers' small plane got off the ground in 1903.

Everyone knows about the Wright brothers, but far fewer people know the name of the man who built and maintained their plane: Charles E. Taylor. He was the first aircraft mechanic, or, as they are called today, aircraft maintenance technician (AMT). Without Charles Taylor, the Wright brothers could never have gotten off the ground—or landed safely.

Flying isn't only about wonder and beauty. It's also a multibillion dollar business and an important mode of transportation. According to the Federal Aviation Administration (FAA), air travel is the safest, most efficient method of transportation in the United States today. While Orville and Wilbur Wright were a passenger list of two back in 1903, ninety-seven years later, in 2000, nearly 700 million passengers flew safely on commercial airplanes within the United States—and that doesn't count the millions more who flew internationally. The number is constantly increasing, too.

This book gives you the facts about aircraft maintenance, from the different certificates that AMTs can obtain, to career opportunities in different types of aviation. You will learn about FAA-certified schools, education, and testing requirements, and the professional organizations that provide support. You will also learn how to apply for a job, a little bit about what it's like to train to be an aircraft maintenance technician, and what happens day to day on the job.

According to Bill O'Brien, aircraft mechanic and aviation safety inspector for the FAA, "When you step outside and see a pair of shiny wings at altitude, the glint off those wings is a tribute to the pilot whose skill took it there. The white line behind those shiny wings is the autograph of the mechanics whose maintenance skills keep it there."

If you like working with your hands, have mechanical aptitude, enjoy problem solving, and/or love aviation and flying, then a career in aircraft maintenance may be for you.

Aviation, Aviation Mechanics, and Avionics Professionals

Few professions have changed the way aircraft maintenance has. That very first AMT, Charles Taylor, built a simple combustion engine that got the Wright brothers' plane off the ground at Kitty Hawk, North Carolina. Today, the Wright brothers' flight could take off and land inside the 150-foot economy passengers' section of a Boeing 747-400. Mr. Taylor himself could sit inside a modern jet engine as he worked on it, just as the AMTs of today do.

Who Employs Aircraft Maintenance Technicians?

Large commercial air carriers are the airlines that we are all familiar with, including American Airlines, United Airlines, and Delta Airlines. In 2000, more than 4,000 passenger jets carried approximately 700 million passengers. The Federal Aviation Administration estimates that passengers,

In 1903, Orville *(left)* and Wilbur Wright made the first sustained flight of an airplane. Their flying machine is pictured above.

planes, and profits, which can range from $10 million to more than $100 million annually, will continue to increase in number. By 2011, the FAA predicts the airlines will serve a staggering one billion passengers a year. The number of planes required will increase to more than 6,400 during the same period, and this will provide increased work for aircraft maintenance technicians.

Right now, major commercial airlines employ approximately 60,000 AMTs at terminals and overhaul bases throughout the United States and overseas. Overhaul bases are facilities where jets are flown in order to undergo scheduled maintenance before they are allowed back into flight. AMTs who work on jets for the major airlines generally earn more than their counterparts who work for other types of aviation companies or on other types of aircraft. They earned an average of $23.25 an hour in 2000.

If you work for a major airline, it is likely that you will start at an overhaul base before you are assigned to an airport terminal, so that you can learn all about the airline's specific aircraft and maintenance procedures.

Overhaul centers are located in:

✔ Atlanta, Georgia

✔ Denver, Colorado

✔ Kansas City, Missouri

✔ Minneapolis, Minnesota

✔ New York, New York

✔ Los Angeles, California

✔ San Francisco, California

✔ Tulsa, Oklahoma

After AMTs gain experience working at an overhaul base, they can "bid out" to transfer to work at the line station of their choice. Line stations are located at every airport the airline services. AMTs who work for a major airline must be willing to travel and relocate, and they should also be willing to do shift work. Major airlines operate twenty-four hours a day, and so do their AMTs and other maintenance personnel.

Instead of working for a major commercial airline, AMTs may work directly for aircraft manufacturers, such as Boeing or the Airbus Consortium. Most United States aircraft assemblers and manufacturers are located in the traditional aerospace centers of California or Washington state.

The second major category of employment for aircraft maintenance technicians is called general aviation. This broad category includes everything from $35 million privately owned corporate jets to radial engine-powered agricultural planes (crop dusters), and every other type of aircraft in between. About 37,000 mechanics were employed in general aviation in 2000.

In addition to working for private aircraft owners, small regional airports, and other commercial aviation businesses, general aviation mechanics can work in one of the repair stations authorized by the FAA. There, they will work on a variety of aircraft brought in for repairs that meet FAA standards. AMTs who work in general aviation often earn less than their counterparts who work for major airlines, but shift work is not essential in this field. The average hourly pay of an AMT in general aviation was $16.50 an hour in 2000, according to *Aircraft Maintenance Technology* magazine.

The third major employer of aircraft mechanics is the federal government. Many people are not aware that thousands of civilians work on military aircraft for the army, navy, marines, and air force. AMTs who work for the military may be employed at bases in the United States or overseas. Like AMTs who work for major commercial airlines, mechanics employed by the armed forces may be asked to work different shifts, or to perform overtime work as needed.

In addition to the armed forces, the FAA itself employs mechanics, especially at its main overhaul base in Oklahoma City, Oklahoma, where AMTs work in the FAA's flight inspection program. AMTs working for the FAA can also gain additional experience and become certified as aviation inspectors, traveling across the United States to ensure safety and standards.

Local and state governments also employ mechanics to maintain their official aircraft, from police helicopters to medical and search-and-rescue planes.

Almost half of all aircraft mechanics are members of a union, whether or not they are employed by a major airline. These unions help to

A military aircraft mechanic prepares a plane for flight.

ensure standards, fair pay and benefits, and good employment conditions.

History of Aircraft Maintenance

Aircraft mechanics performed a vital role in keeping planes in the air during both World War I and World War II, and in Vietnam, the Gulf War, and other military conflicts. In fact, since 1903, aircraft maintenance mechanics have been responsible for all aspects of the aircraft's airworthiness. Airworthiness is a plane's ability to fly safely and well.

Early aircraft engines were simple four-stroke internal combustion engines that drove the propeller shaft, providing the airplane with the thrust to get into the air. Early aircraft frames were made of wood covered in cloth. This cloth was painted with a special paint that dried to a hard, smooth finish, stabilizing the wings and providing an aerodynamic surface. This paint was called "dope" and variations of it are still used today on the wings of small, propeller-driven aircraft. In fact, many early planes have been restored and are still in flight thanks to antique aircraft enthusiasts and the mechanics who have preserved the tradition of these magnificent flying machines.

In-line and radial combustion engines like the ones that the early aircraft mechanics worked on are still being used in small aircraft today. If you are familiar with automobile engines, you will recognize many small aircraft engines as being similar to the engine in your car.

Piston-driven engines require a lot of maintenance, and they also use lubricants such as oil and grease. Mechanics who worked on these engines couldn't help but get these lubricants on their hands and clothes. Because of this, early mechanics were called "grease monkeys," though that is very much a term of the past. As one Northwest Airlines AMT says, "I very seldom get dirty on the job. Most of the work on the new types of aircraft is electrical and very clean."

One of the major changes in AMTs' daily work came with the introduction of the turbojet in 1939. The turbojet is the engine that is used in large commercial and most military jet aircraft. It involves far fewer moving parts than any piston-driven engine. The most powerful jet engines of today, such as GE's GE-90, provide up to 115,000 pounds of thrust, which is far more powerful than the few thousand pounds of thrust provided by the early jet engines. The jet engines that power today's huge commercial aircraft are large enough for AMTs to stand in them.

Another major change in aviation has been the increased emphasis on safety—and safety has always been the primary concern of the aircraft mechanic. Ideas about safety in flying have changed over the years. However, pilots were not required to have a license to fly in the United States until 1926, and before the first three air traffic control towers were built at airports in 1936, pilots avoided other aircraft by a method called "see and be seen." That could never work today.

Today, aircraft mechanics work on the entire range of aviation maintenance needs, from small, one-seat piston-powered airplanes to the jumbo jets of our modern airlines and high-tech military aircraft. Space-age technology has changed the "grease monkeys" of the past into experts who can troubleshoot complex electronic navigation systems as well as tighten a bolt or pack wheel bearings.

Today's aviation mechanics perform to the highest standards of excellence and safety. FAA inspector Bill O'Brien says, "A mechanic must be 99.9 percent right all of the time. He or she is not allowed a margin for error, no second chances, and no excuses for failure, even if the windchill factor was five below zero and passengers are waiting."

Just as the Wright brothers flew and landed safely thanks to the mechanical skills of Charles E. Taylor, thousands of today's pilots take off and land worry-free because of the mechanics whose training, dedication, and professionalism keep their planes in the air. Aircraft maintenance technicians know that hundreds of millions of lives depend upon their work, and this produces the sense of pride and accomplishment that is a hallmark of their profession.

Job Classifications and FAA Certification

Aircraft maintenance technicians work in the only maintenance profession that is certified by the federal government—since so many lives depend on their work. As you learn more about aircraft

An A & P mechanic from Northwest Airlines works on an engine at the line maintenance hangar at Detroit Metropolitan Airport in Romulus, Michigan.

maintenance, you will often hear the term "A & P mechanic" or "A & P certificate." There are actually two certificates and ratings provided by the FAA, one for Airframe (A) skills, and one for powerplant (P) skills. Most certified mechanics hold both ratings, and they are called A & P mechanics. However, some mechanics are only certificated with an airframe or a powerplant rating, making them only A or only P mechanics.

A & P mechanics perform tasks that include adjusting, aligning, and calibrating aircraft systems, and use hand tools, gauges, and computerized equipment. One of the most important jobs that they perform is inspecting engines or other mechanical components for cracks, wear, or leaks, and repairing them, if necessary. As part of scheduled maintenance, they test engine and system operations using special testing equipment. If there are any problems detected, they must be able to disassemble and inspect, then repair or replace all parts of the aircraft, from the inside out.

They service and maintain all of the aircraft's systems, from flushing crankcases to greasing moving parts and checking the brakes. They must even be able to remove the engine from the aircraft or install a new engine. Since some aircraft engines are extremely large, this is a demanding, highly technical task. They use forklifts and engine slings and stands while they are performing this aspect of their work.

Airframe and powerplant mechanics rely upon aircraft maintenance manuals and FAA publications to assist them in determining proper repair and inspection procedures. They work on the structure of the aircraft as well, including its wings, fuselage, flight controls, and landing gear. They even have been known to change a plane's tire!

Airframe and powerplant mechanics may also perform modifications on aircrafts according to engineering plans and specifications. Some A & P mechanics work at stations that do nothing but modify aircraft for specialized purposes, such as converting passenger jets to cargo aircraft.

Mechanics who do not have their A & P certificates, but who are certified for specific tasks, are called repairmen. Repairmen are certified by the FAA for only one or two specific tasks. Because they are limited by function, they work under the supervision of FAA-approved repair stations, commercial operators, or air carriers (airlines), doing the specific tasks they are certified to perform on a routine, daily basis.

In addition to the repairmen, there are non-certified mechanics who may work only under the supervision of an FAA-certified mechanic. These non-certified mechanics usually work in manufacturing, at an FAA repair station, for an air carrier, or for a fixed-base operator (FBO).

Another related field is that of the avionics technician. Avionics technicians hold an airframe rating and certificate, and they also have additional training which allows them to work on some of the most advanced electronic equipment. Avionics technicians often work on the "black boxes" that record flight data, giving safety inspectors crucial clues in case an airplane crashes. Research and development companies may employ someone with this type of training, as well.

Sometimes uncertified employees work for avionics companies or repair stations. They may have gained their experience by working in the military or for avionics manufacturers or other related industries, but they are not officially called avionics technicians or A & P mechanics.

Employment Outlook

Industry experts are forecasting a shortage of 10,000 A & P–rated mechanics over the next five years. Many aircraft maintenance technicians who are currently employed in the field started their jobs during the 1960s. This was a time of rapid growth for the aviation industry, with many advances in technology and a huge increase in the manufacture of commercial as well as military aircraft. Many of the AMTs who started work during the 1960s are now retiring. What's more, fewer AMTs have come into the field from the military in recent years, largely due to cutbacks in the armed forces. The United States Bureau of Labor Statistics says "opportunities should be favorable" for new aircraft maintenance technicians, though competition is likely to be stiff for the higher-paying positions with major airlines. Students who are just beginning training can look forward to good employment opportunities.

However, aspiring aircraft maintenance technicians should also be aware that during economic recession, airlines are often forced to curtail flights. This results in less aircraft maintenance being needed, and sometimes, layoffs for mechanics. But the extensive training and certification that aircraft maintenance technicians receive qualifies them to work in many related fields, such as electronic equipment repair and manufacture, heavy machinery equipment repair, and facilities maintenance. All of these are growing fields, and FAA-certified A & P mechanics are desired by many employers. In some cases, nearly half of the graduates of aircraft maintenance technical programs are working in fields other than aviation maintenance. Some AMTs have even gone to work at amusement parks like Disneyland or Six Flags; the skills they possess can help make high-tech rides safe, just the same as they can for high-tech jet aircrafts.

Still, overall, the future employment picture for aircraft maintenance technicians is bright. A well trained, certified technician with a strong background in technical subjects should have little trouble finding a lifetime career in aviation.

Unions

About half of the aircraft maintenance technicians in the United States are members of one of the aircraft maintenance unions. Their salaries are determined by the negotiations between the unions and major air carriers, manufacturers, or repair stations.

The principal unions are the International Association of Machinists and Aerospace Workers (IAMAW), the Professional Aviation Maintenance Association (PAMA), the Aircraft Mechanics Fraternal Association (AMFA), and the Transport Workers Union of America (TWU). The unions negotiate salaries, working conditions, and health and pension benefits on behalf of their members, as well as conduct educational activities, provide pension and retirement funds, and lobby for political or other causes.

Salaries, Wages, and Benefits

Because aircraft maintenance technicians can work in so many areas, both within and outside the aviation industry, their wages, salaries, and benefits vary.

Aircraft mechanics who start work in general aviation and are employed by small fixed-base operator or FAA-certified repair stations will earn between $18,000 and $24,000 a year. Avionics technicians can earn between $22,000 and $28,000 a year to start.

Major air carriers offer annual starting salaries of between $20,000 and $27,000 to qualified A & P certificate holders. Maintenance is performed around the clock for major air carriers, seven days a week. One experienced mechanic said that mechanics should expect to work nights and weekends until they've put in at least five years of service. Within five years, a mechanic with an A & P certificate should earn between $35,000 and $45,000 a year, and mechanics and their families receive additional benefits, such as reduced-fare air travel.

Avionics technicians may earn between $38,000 and $48,000 a year after five years of service with a major air carrier.

Air carriers also provide paid holidays, vacations, insurance plans (medical, dental, and life), retirement programs, and sick leave. These benefits may not be available at smaller, independent organizations, although some general aviation corporations provide benefit packages that rival or better those offered by major air carriers.

Hourly pay can range from $14 an hour for starting mechanics at small, independent airports, to more than $22 an hour at the major airlines.

Some mechanics prefer to work in general aviation or for independent corporations because most jobs of this type are found at local airports or in smaller cities. The quality of life there is less hectic, and the job hours and duties are less stressful than those of AMTs who work for major airlines at the large, urban hub airports. Experienced mechanics also recommend that new AMTs gain experience in the lower-stress world of general aviation before moving to work for a major airline. The increased experience can lead to higher starting salaries and greater job confidence as well.

How to Get Started

Aircraft maintenance is a profession that requires a true commitment to training and excellence. Because lives depend upon the competency and professionalism of the mechanics, aspiring maintenance mechanics must complete a lot of training, gain experience, and pass written exams, oral tests, and practical tests to receive each of their certifications and ratings. Avionics technicians must also have additional training, experience, and certifications. Even repairmen must take tests and certify their hours of experience in their specialties to obtain certificates.

To meet the most basic job requirements applicants must:

✔ Be eighteen years of age or older

✔ Be able to read, write, and understand English

✔ Document eighteen months of experience in either one of the ratings sought (airframe or powerplant), or thirty months of practical experience working concurrently on airframes and powerplants, or graduation from an FAA-approved Part 147 aviation maintenance technician school

✔ Pass a written examination, an oral test, and a practical test for each rating

✔ Pass all tests within twenty-four months of application

Most aspiring aircraft maintenance technicians can take advantage of the more than 200 FAA-approved schools across the United States. These schools offer training that enables students to get practical experience and to pass their tests.

Aspiring AMTs can choose one of three paths to get the experience they need to receive their FAA airframe and powerplant certificates and become A & P mechanics.

Working at a Maintenance Facility

An individual can work under the supervision of an A & P mechanic at an FAA-approved repair station or a fixed-base operator for eighteen months for each individual certificate, or thirty months for both ratings. A month of practical experience contains at least 160 hours of documented work. This work experience must be documented by either pay stubs, a log book signed by the supervising mechanic, or a notarized statement of work hours, also signed by the supervising mechanic. Additional

25

study time is also required to prepare for the series of FAA examinations.

Military Service

Individuals can join one of the United States armed services and enter a military occupational specialty (MOS) that is credited by the FAA for practical experience for the mechanic certificates. If you are interested in choosing this option for gaining experience, check with your local FAA flight standards district office (FSDO) and get a current list of the acceptable MOS codes that will give you the experience you need to qualify for your airframe and powerplant ratings. The same number of months of practical experience (eighteen months for a single rating, thirty months for the combined A & P rating) is required and must be certified by the applicant's executive officer, maintenance officer, or classification officer. Additional study time is required for military service personnel, as well.

FAA-Approved Aviation Maintenance Schools

There are about 200 FAA Part 147–approved aircraft maintenance schools in the United States. These schools offer all of the training and experience required to obtain the airframe and powerplant ratings. They also offer courses leading to certificates in avionics, electronics, and instrumentation. Most schools require a high school diploma. The length of the courses varies from twelve to twenty-four months, but in-school training is always shorter than

Pima Community College students rivet the fuselage of an airplane at the JobPath aircraft maintenance training facility in Tucson, Arizona.

the on-the-job training requirements of eighteen to thirty months.

Attending aircraft maintenance school is demanding. There are a few schools that will graduate students and prepare them for their FAA exams in only one year, but most programs take two years—twenty-four months or four semesters. At San Bernardino Valley College in southern California, students acquire their mandatory 1,900 hours of practical experience while attending classes and workshops. They study every night— most students carry their manuals with them wherever they go. For the first two semesters, aspiring mechanics are at the school seven hours a day, while for the last two semesters they attend classes three to four hours a day and work on independent projects. In addition, they are preparing for their written, oral, and practical exams. If they pass, an FAA inspector will award them their airframe and powerplant certificates.

The most important skills that aspiring aircraft maintenance technicians learn are in the areas of problem solving and deductive reasoning, sometimes called troubleshooting. For example, an instructor might hand a student technician a dozen parts and ask him or her to identify what they are made of, their part numbers, and what their use is in the airplane.

Students use inspection equipment, measuring equipment, FAA-approved maintenance manuals, and their own experience to complete such tasks. They also take apart and rebuild every type of aircraft engine—from simple piston engines to big turbojets—and they work on all aspects of aircraft systems. They may even recover and paint the cloth wings of an old-fashioned propeller-driven airplane to learn the basics of aerodynamics and air-worthiness. All schools have working airplanes, helicopters, and equipment so that students gain hands-on experience.

While at aviation school, aspiring AMTs can not only gain education and experience for their airframe and powerplant certificates, but they can also get experience in and special certificates for working with composites, nondestructive testing, computers, electronics, and avionics. All of this experience and these special certificates contribute to students finding better-paying jobs and having more employment options after graduation and certification.

Aviation maintenance students install tracking and balancing sensors on a UH-1 "Huey" at Clover Park Technical College in Tacoma, Washington.

Some AMTs even get their pilot's licenses as well. As one AMT said, "I might as well learn to fly them if I know how to take them apart and build them."

Preparing for the FAA exams takes a lot of time. Students, whether they are gaining practical work experience through the private sector (or the military) or attending an FAA-approved school, study two to three hours a night. "I carry my books every day so that I can do the work," said B. J. Stickle, who has already earned her airframe rating and is now working on her powerplant certificate.

After graduating from aircraft maintenance school, most students return to take their written, oral, and practical exams from an FAA-certified examiner, who is also an FAA air safety inspector. The best advice that AMTs, students, and instructors can give is to study regularly and to be rested and refreshed on the day of your exams. They also say that after all of the practical experience and aviation maintenance training these schools provide, aspiring mechanics should easily pass these exams. Sample test booklets for the oral and practical exams in general aviation, airframe, and power-plant certification, sample exam questions, and sample preparation manuals are available from the FAA and industry publishers like Jeppesen, McGraw-Hill, and ASA. These are very familiar to aircraft maintenance students because they are the books that they use throughout their training and in all of their courses.

After graduation, students are qualified to take the FAA examinations. Some students elect to complete one rating area first (airframe or powerplant) and continue with their training, rather than taking both exams at the same time. According to Bill O'Brien of the FAA, graduates of the approved training schools can start work at higher salaries than individuals who earn their certifications based strictly on military or civilian work experience.

After you finish your training and pass the series of FAA exams, you will need to set up a toolbox in order to start work. Nearly all mechanics provide their own tools. Allen Moore, professor in the aeronautics program at San Bernardino Valley College in California, says that a start-up tool kit usually costs between $500 and $1,000.

Getting a Job

Because there are so many areas of aviation that employ aircraft maintenance technicians, there are many ways to get a good job. Completing your training at an FAA-approved school and obtaining A & P certificates and ratings are significant achievements, and prospective employers recognize this.

Aircraft mechanics usually contact employers directly, either in person or by résumé. Individual employers include commercial airlines, aircraft and parts manufacturers, aircraft service and maintenance companies, corporations with fleets of planes, government organizations, and the military. Most aircraft maintenance schools have an active job placement service, and most AMTs get their first job through referrals from their school. Other sources for job information include newspaper classified advertisements, professional publications such as *Aircraft Maintenance Technology* magazine, or Web pages devoted to aviation. Sometimes, state employment development offices provide information on local jobs in aircraft maintenance, and private employment agencies may be able to provide information as well.

Some employers are now using a five-step interview process for prospective employees that includes a written test, an oral test, a practical test, the traditional job interview, and even a personality profile. Safety requirements and what AMTs refer to as the "human factor," meaning a mechanic's judgment and attitude on the job, are crucial for the AMT's success on the job. The personality test helps to determine if you've got what it takes to be a successful aircraft maintenance professional. When you go to a job interview, be prepared to provide your certificates and have your exam results ready. For practical exams, have your tools and be ready to show your stuff and do the work.

An A & P mechanic's training and preparation for a wide range of mechanical tasks is well-known. In some areas, as many as 50 percent of mechanics with A & P certificates are working in industries that are not directly connected with airplanes or airports because their skills are highly desirable to many employers, both within and outside the field of aviation.

Now You're on the Job

What kind of a person is an aircraft mechanic? You don't have to talk to very many aircraft maintenance professionals before you discover how much they love airplanes, flying, and working with their hands. Allen Moore, professor at the aircraft maintenance school in San Bernardino, California, says, "Aviation isn't just a career or a profession . . . it's a disease."

Bill O'Brien, aircraft mechanic and inspector for the FAA, says that it's hard to explain the marriage of human feelings and technology that is the essential ingredient of the aircraft maintenance profession. While pilots are in love with the freedom of flight, AMTs "carry on a technological love affair with the aircraft itself," he says. This love affair is complex because it involves hard numbers, close tolerances, and no margin for error. This combination of emotion and technology is hard to put into words, according to O'Brien. "How can I explain the feeling that a mechanic

An FAA aviation safety inspector performs a walkaround inspection of a commercial jet. Almost all aviation safety inspectors are A & P certified mechanics.

has when he takes a sick aircraft and puts it back in the air again?" he asks, and then adds, "No one sings songs or writes poetry about mechanics and their profession."

But that is not precisely true. There is one poem that has been written about aircraft mechanics. It's called "The Forgotten Man." The poem is old, and the author is unknown, but part of the poem reads:

Now pilots are highly trained people
And wings are not easily won.
But without the work of the maintenance man
Our pilots would march with a gun.

So when you see the mighty jet aircraft
As they mark their path through the air,
The grease-stained man with the wrench in
    his hand
Is the man who put them there.

Most aircraft mechanics make poetry with their hands, and they see the results of their work in the thousands of shining planes that safely take off and land each day at airports across America. Their poetry is the poetry of flight. Aircraft mechanics have also written their own creed, which says in part:

Knowing full well that the safety and lives of others are dependent upon my skill and judgment, I will never knowingly subject others to risks which I would not be willing to assume for myself, or for those dear to me.

The serious responsibility of maintaining constant good judgment and skill, having "no margin for error and no room for mistakes," as Bill O'Brien says, means that aircraft maintenance is—as can't be repeated too often—not a stress-free occupation. Aircraft mechanics often work long hours. Especially with major air carriers and at major repair stations, AMTs can expect to work a lot of overtime. They cannot rush their jobs: Safety must always come first. Because of this, experienced mechanics strongly urge young mechanics to gain several years of experience in the less stressful environment of general aviation before venturing out to work for the majors.

While any AMT can choose to work at his or her local airport in general aviation, you can have a great future and career if you're willing to relocate.

Women in Aircraft Maintenance

While both men and women work as aircraft maintenance technicians, women are still a minority in the profession—but their numbers are on the increase. The Association for Women in Aviation estimates that 1.3 percent of current AMTs are female, but nearly 10 percent of current aircraft maintenance students are female. Like many male AMTs, female AMTs often come from aviation families, with fathers and grandfathers who have worked in the profession, either as pilots, mechanics, or in other aspects of aviation.

Because the field of aircraft maintenance was almost exclusively male in the past, with the famous exception of "Rosie the Riveter" during World War II, women have been thought of as "distractions" on the job. But with increasing participation from both genders, and with the help of groups like the Association for Women in Aviation and the Association for Women in Aviation Maintenance (AWAM), this perception is changing.

One Person's Story

B. J. Stickle is a southern Californian who has already received her airframe (A) rating, and is working toward her powerplant (P) certification.

I like the challenge of aircraft maintenance. Without a challenge, you can never learn. I was always good with my hands, and I loved working with machines. My grandfather worked for Boeing from the first day they opened to the day he retired. I look at it this way: I'm getting a license to learn.

Every time I get to work, I learn a hundred new things every day. I never understood the intricacies of aircrafts before, all of the details and the fine points. Now, it's a challenge that I want to meet.

You have to be self-motivated and hardworking to do this type of work. You don't know what problems are going to come up, and if you're the type of person I am, that's exactly what you want to do every day.

It's like a lot of jobs where women haven't been involved in the past. You have to be twice as good as the man to be accepted. But that's OK. If they outdo me or outperform me, then they can look down on me. But so far, that hasn't happened.

The Work Environment

Most mechanics and avionics technicians work in hangars, on flight lines, or in repair stations located in or near major airports. They use hand tools and power tools as well as sophisticated electronic and computerized testing equipment. The noise level both inside a hangar and on the flight line can be very high. As one experienced AMT warns, "You need to wear your ear plugs. Otherwise, you could lose your hearing."

Mechanics who work flight line maintenance can often work in all kinds of weather and temperatures, although the temperature and environment are much better controlled in maintenance facilities and assembly plants. Aircraft maintenance is a job for people who are physically fit, because they must perform moderate to heavy physical activities. They are commonly asked to lift up to fifty pounds, and they can be asked to lift items weighing seventy pounds or more.

From climbing ladders to crawling under wings and into tight, confining engine or under-plane areas, mechanics must also be agile and

An avionics technician tests the rudder of a Boeing 737 during a National Transportation Safety Board investigation of the crash of a similar plane.

flexible. Although the mechanics of today seldom get as "greasy" as mechanics did in the past, and although a lot of work is done with computerized testing equipment and complex and delicate electronic components, mechanics can still get dirty. Airplanes still have tires and hydraulic landing gear, and even planes with jet engines have parts that need to be cleaned and lubricated.

For major air carriers and many maintenance facilities, as well as the military, work continues twenty-four hours a day, seven days a week. Maintenance mechanics may work day, swing, or night shifts (commonly known as the graveyard shift). At many commercial airlines, overtime is the rule, not the exception, though many AMTs appreciate the additional income that overtime work provides.

It's not all hard work, however. A Northwest Airlines mechanic says, "One of the fun things that we get to do, that the public doesn't realize, is to taxi the aircraft around the airport when we are working on the flight line."

So, if you are an AMT working for a major airline, chances are you may be able to learn how to "drive" a jumbo jet, after you make sure that everything is in perfect working order.

FAA and airline safety requirements also mean that AMTs must adhere to the same drug-free standards as other flight personnel, such as pilots and flight engineers. Major airlines have instituted drug-testing programs. Usually, 10 percent of employees are selected at random each quarter for drug testing. They are given a urine test by a supervisor. If AMTs test positive for narcotics or other controlled substances, their employment will be terminated.

Mechanics who work in general aviation usually have much more flexibility in their work hours and schedules than AMTs who work for airlines or major repair facilities. Pay is not as high in general aviation as it is for those who work for a major airline, but the stress factor is also lower. AMTs who work for major airlines work on strict time schedules. They are asked to complete maintenance tasks, sometimes in a very limited period of time, because flight schedules must be maintained. According to one AMT with twenty years of experience, "If you like to take your time and don't like a lot of pressure, then general aviation is for you."

If you work for a major airline or a repair station, you can work in several different specialty areas. Some repair specialists troubleshoot and fix problems with the aircraft, working closely with pilots and flight engineers. Others specialize as airframe or powerplant mechanics, using the specific skills obtained through their training and FAA certification. Flight line mechanics perform FAA and airline-mandated checks each day at an airport, working on each aircraft that comes in through the flight line. With experience, AMTs can become lead mechanics, supervising a crew of other AMTs, shop supervisors, and even directors of maintenance and maintenance managers, overseeing several different crews and aspects of maintenance operation. Other areas of specialty include helicopter maintenance and avionics.

Advancement

AMTs have the opportunity to advance to lead mechanic, shop supervisor, and, eventually, director of maintenance or maintenance manager. Some AMTs acquire further training and education and qualify to be inspectors, working either for the FAA or for the airlines themselves. In many aircraft maintenance programs, AMTs have the opportunity to obtain an Associate of Science degree in aeronautics or aviation maintenance. Instructors strongly urge aspiring mechanics to consider this option, which can usually be obtained through taking only a few additional general education courses in addition to the core program in aviation maintenance and obtaining their airframe and powerplant ratings and certificates. If you have completed your training course and have qualified for your A & P certificates, you already have more than half the credits needed for a two-year degree.

Advancement beyond the level of lead mechanic or shop supervisor usually means that AMTs will need a four-year college degree. Promotion in the ever-changing aviation environment depends upon having something better than your competitor. That "something better" is a certificate in an area of specialty, such as avionics, electronics, composites, computers, or various types of testing.

AMTs can obtain additional training through many different sources, including the 200 FAA-approved training schools across the United States and specialized courses conducted through the FAA itself. They can also obtain Bachelor of Science degrees through any accredited school. Often, accredited institutions will give the AMT credit for work experience, helping greatly toward obtaining the degree. If you do choose to obtain a bachelor's degree, remember that the education and training you've already gone through to get your airframe and powerplant certificates is extensive. Most college degrees require 1,600 hours in the classroom, while FAA-approved aircraft maintenance programs put students through 1,900 hours of training in forty-three different subject areas, and AMTs must pass nine FAA exams in order to obtain their ratings. FAA Inspector O'Brien says, "Don't ever think that you're just a mechanic. You'll be working on aircrafts worth $35 million or more! I'm not aware of any two-year or four-year college program that even comes close to having the number of courses that someone with an A & P certificate must successfully complete. If you do choose to get a two- or four-year college degree after you get A & P certificates, don't let the cost scare you away. An education lasts a lifetime. When you think that it costs less than half of what a brand-new car or truck costs, it's quite a bargain."

Related Careers in Aviation

In addition to the many different opportunities available to aircraft maintenance technicians, there are many other fascinating jobs in the world of aviation.

Aircraft Manufacturing

The major divisions within the aircraft manufacturing industry are airframe, flight controls, accessory and equipment, and engine. Workers are needed in all of these divisions.

Technicians

Technicians can specialize in repairing and testing aircraft as they are being manufactured. This job category also includes drafters and technical writers and illustrators.

Aerospace Workers

Aerospace workers engage in metal work, composite fabrication, machinery and tool fabrication,

The rear fuselage section of a Boeing 757-300 is lifted into place at a factory in Renton, Washington. AMTs test and repair aircraft as they are being manufactured.

assembly and installation, inspecting and testing (quality control), and many other jobs.

Flying Careers

There are about 17,500 airports in the United States and approximately 4,000 heliports, but did you know that only about 680 airports are served by airlines? All of the other airports are used for general aviation pilots and their planes.

Pilots

Some AMTs do obtain their pilot's licenses, while some pilots gain training as aircraft mechanics in order to work on their own planes.

For many professional pilots, the ultimate job is to be an airline captain. The pay can be very good—

top salary at some of the higher paying major airlines is around $160,000 a year. Most airline pilots start out as first officer (copilot) with a regional carrier; initially they earn about $12,000 to $18,000 a year. And when they join a major airline, their first position may not be as a pilot, but as a flight engineer.

In addition to airline pilot, other pilot jobs include flight instructor, corporate pilot, charter pilot, test pilot, and agricultural pilot.

Nonflying Airline Careers

Most airline jobs require a high school diploma. All workers, regardless of their jobs, are given some degree of on-the-job training. There are even some private technical schools that offer training. You will find that schools that specialize in aircraft maintenance programs may have other programs that lead to other types of airline careers, either in the air or on the ground.

Station Manager or Agent

This position is found at smaller, regional airports. The station manager is responsible for all flight and ground operations, such as aircraft handling, passenger services, and air cargo operations. The manager may also sell tickets, make public announcements, check in baggage, and perform other needed services.

Other Jobs

Airlines and airports employ food service employees, ramp planners, and ramp personnel (they drive food trucks, move mobile stairs, maintain air conditioning units, and drive messenger cars and employee transport buses). Other jobs include auto mechanic, cabin maintenance mechanics, and administrative personnel. Salaries in the airline industry are generally above the average paid by other types of industries and businesses.

Government Careers

People who are interested in aviation can choose to work for the government as opposed to private businesses, airlines, and airports.

United States Military Services

One of the major employment sectors is the United States armed forces. The United States Air Force offers the greatest number of opportunities to fly as a pilot or work as an aircraft mechanic, air traffic controller, technician, flight nurse, or meteorological technician, to name a few of the thousands of jobs that are available.

The other three branches of the armed forces, the United States Army, Navy, and Marine Corps, offer jobs similar to those available in the air force. army aviation is focused on the operation of its helicopters and subsonic light planes (reconnaissance aircraft). The United States Coast Guard operates search and rescue aircraft. Many military aviation jobs, including aircraft mechanics, are good preparation for similar jobs in the civilian sector.

FAA Jobs

The Federal Aviation Administration, as well as state and local governments, also provide related employment opportunities.

Air Traffic Controllers

Air traffic control specialists work at FAA airport traffic control towers, directing traffic so that it flows smoothly, safely, and efficiently. They give pilots taxiing, takeoff, and landing instructions.

Other FAA jobs

The FAA also employs electronics technicians, aviation safety inspectors (all are usually A & P-certified mechanics), aerospace system inspection pilots, flight test pilots, engineering technicians, and airport safety specialists.

Other Federal Jobs

Some of the agencies that use aircraft and employ skilled aviation personnel include the National Aeronautics and Space Administration (NASA), the National Transportation Safety Board (NTSB), and the National Weather Service. There are also many federal services, such as the Fish and Wildlife Service of the Department of the Interior, or the Forest Service of the Department of Agriculture. Almost every state has an aeronautics department or commission. Pilots, field service representatives, safety officers, and aircraft

U.S. Marine Corps corporal Nathan Webb prepares to work on a Marine Harrier attack jet in a hangar at Cherry Point Marine Corps Air Station in North Carolina.

mechanics are employed by various states. Local governments maintain a wide range of aircraft that are used by law enforcement agencies, and for firefighting, search and rescue, and a broad range of other purposes, such as surveying and transporting government personnel to far-flung areas to perform their duties.

Careers for Mechanics Outside of Aviation

By the time you have qualified to be an aircraft mechanic, you possess skills that are important in many different industries. Jobs are available in virtually every industry that uses or manufactures equipment and machinery. Nearly half of the recent graduates of the aircraft maintenance school in San Bernardino, California, are working outside of the aviation industry. Starting salaries for A & P mechanics are higher than starting salaries for mechanics who lack these certificates.

Maintenance Electricians

These electricians spend much of their time in preventive maintenance. They periodically inspect equipment, and locate and correct problems before breakdowns occur. Jobs are available in the automotive industry, local government, and manufacturing.

Maintenance Machinists

Also called industrial machinery repairers, these workers troubleshoot and repair heavy machinery

A NASA technician makes his way down the stairs after making repairs to the uppermost level near the space shuttle *Atlantis*'s external fuel tank.

in factories. Although repair work is the industrial machinery mechanics' most important job, they also perform preventive maintenance.

Automotive Mechanics (and Related Fields)

Automotive mechanics diagnose, troubleshoot, and repair cars. They can work independently, or for automotive dealers or private repair shops. Related fields of expertise include motorcycle mechanics, diesel mechanics, farm machinery mechanics, and boat/marine engine mechanics.

General Maintenance

General maintenance mechanics can work virtually anywhere, from schools and hospitals to large office buildings and amusement parks. They inspect and diagnose problems in a wide range of areas, and determine the best way to correct them. They also perform preventive maintenance.

Conclusion

As you can see from this book, the profession of aircraft mechanic is exciting, challenging, and rewarding. With pride in their achievements, the aircraft mechanics of today can look toward a bright future in the ever-changing world of aviation. AMTs make sure that millions of people fly safely every day across the United States and the world. As aircraft manufacturing and air transport grows ever more sophisticated, AMTs can look forward to continued work with high-tech machinery and electronics. In

AMTs are involved in almost every stage of the aircraft building process—from assembly and installation to quality control.

the future, they may even troubleshoot and repair commercial vehicles headed for high Earth orbit, the Moon, or even beyond, as aviation moves into the twenty-first century.

Glossary

A & P mechanic Mechanic who has completed the training and practical experience in the airframe (A) and powerplant (P) aspects of maintaining and repairing aircraft, and who has passed all FAA examinations in these areas.

aerodynamics Science and technology of flight.

aeronautics Field of education, work, and study related to flight and aviation.

aircraft maintenance technicians (AMTs) Individuals who perform maintenance, repair, and assembly duties on aircrafts, from single-engine planes to jumbo jets and helicopters.

air hub City with a major airport and repair facility.

airworthiness Ability of an aircraft to fly safely due to correct functioning in all respects, from the engine to the exterior.

aviation Business and practice of flying airplanes and other craft, including helicopters.

avionics Specialized field of aircraft manufacturing, maintenance, and testing that involves electronic equipment, such as the "black boxes" that record all flight data.

commercial air carriers Airlines and transport companies that carry passengers and cargo from one of the 680 major airports in the United States.

FAA circular Official publications of the Federal Aviation Administration (FAA) that cover all aspects of the aviation industry.

FAA Part 147–approved schools Two hundred schools in the United States that are officially approved by the FAA to provide education, training, and testing for aircraft maintenance technicians.

fixed base operators (FBOs) Retail firms that sell general aviation products and services at an airport.

flight controls Equipment that provides lift and directional stability of aircraft for takeoff, flying, and landing.

flight line Part of a major airport or military base where planes are maintained and inspected.

flight standards district office (FSDO) Local office of the FAA that oversees testing and safety inspections for aircraft maintenance technicians.

general aviation Term for all aviation activities that are not connected with major airlines or the United States government.

human factor Term used by aircraft mechanics to refer to a mechanic's attitude and judgment in relation to repair and maintenance duties.

inspector Employee of the FAA or an airline who is expert in all areas of maintenance, safety, and government regulations. Usually an A & P mechanic with years of experience who has obtained additional training and education. Inspectors also test mechanics for their airframe (A) and powerplant (P) ratings.

lead mechanic Experienced mechanic who supervises a group of other mechanics.

line mechanic Mechanic who works on a flight or assembly line.

maintenance manager Mechanic who supervises and runs an entire maintenance department, either for an airline repair station or a repair hub.

overhaul bases Repair facilities for major commercial air carriers, located in large cities and regional air centers.

repairman Mechanic who is certified by the FAA to perform specific maintenance duties under the supervision of an A & P-certified mechanic.

shift work Division of a twenty-four-hour work day into three eight-hour shifts, usually called day, swing, and night (or graveyard) shifts.

shop supervisor Mechanic who supervises a facility that repairs aircraft.

troubleshooting Deductive reasoning that all aircraft mechanics must learn, including

methods of determining mechanical problems
and fixing them.

turbojet Method of propulsion for all large
aircraft today. Turbojets use turbines and air
compression, and they burn aircraft fuel to
provide lift so that the plane can take off
and fly.

For More Information

In the United States

Aircraft Mechanics Fraternal Association (AMFA)
67 Water Street, Suite 208 A
Laconia, NH 03246
(603) 527-9212
Web site: http://www.amfanatl.org

Association for Women in Aviation
   Maintenance (AWAM)
P.O. Box 1030
Edgewater, FL 32132-1030
(386) 424-5780
Web site: http://www.awam.org

Federal Aviation Administration (FAA)
800 Independence Avenue SW
Washington, DC 20591
(800) 322-7873
Web site: http://www.faa.gov

International Association of Machinists and
  Aerospace Workers (IAMAW)
9000 Machinists Place
Upper Marlboro, MD 20772-2687
(301) 967-4500
Web site: http://www.iamaw.org

Professional Aviation Maintenance
  Association (PAMA)
1707 H Street NW, Suite 700
Washington, DC 20006-3915
(202) 730-0260
Web site: http://www.pama.org

Transport Workers Union of America (TWU)
80 West End Avenue
New York, NY 10023
(212) 873-6000
Web site: http://www.twu.org

U.S. Department of Transportation
400 Seventh Street, SW
Washington, DC 20590
(800) 525-2878
Web site: http://www.dot.gov
A free list of FAA Certificated aviation maintenance
  technician schools (Advisory Circular 147-2W)
  is available.

In Canada

Transport Canada
Maintenance and Manufacturing (AARP)
330 Sparks Street, 2nd Floor
Place de Ville, Tower C
Ottawa, ON K1A 0N5
(613) 952-1018
Web site: http://www.tc.gc.ca

Web Sites

Federal Aviation Administration
   Career Opportunities
http://jobs.faa.gov/

United States Office of Personnel Management
http://www.usajobs.opm.gov/

For Further Reading

A & P Technician General, Airframe and Powerplant Textbook Kit. Denver, CO: Jeppesen Publishing, 2001.

A & P Technician General Study Guide. Denver, CO: Jeppesen Publishing, 2001.

A & P Technician General Workbook. Denver, CO: Jeppesen Publishing, 2001.

Doganis, Rigas. *The Airline Business in the 21st Century.* New York: Routledge, 2001.

FAA Textbook Set: *General, Airframe and Powerplant* [set of three]. Washington, DC: Federal Aviation Administration, 2000.

Lombardo, David. *Aircraft Systems.* 2nd ed. New York: McGraw Hill Professional Publishing, 1999.

O'Brien, Bill. *An Overview of the Maintenance Profession* (FAA Circular #65-30). Washington, DC: Federal Aviation Administration, 2000.

Reithmaier, Larry, ed. *Standard Aircraft Handbook for Mechanics and Technicians.* 6th ed. New York: McGraw-Hill Professional Publishing, 1999.

Thurston, David B. *The World's Most Significant and Magnificent Aircraft: Evolution of the Modern Airplane.* Warrendale, PA: Society of Automotive Engineers, 2000.

Index

About the Author

Amy Sterling Casil lives in southern California. Her husband is an industrial mechanic. She also writes science fiction and teaches at Chapman University in Orange, California.

Photo Credits

Cover and pp. 2, 9, 13, 34 © Index Stock; pp. 17, 27, 29, 39, 45, 49, 51, 53 © Associated Press.

Design

Geri Giordano

Layout

Nelson Sá